THE DUKE'S CHRISTMAS SCANDAL

HOW THE RAKE STOLE CHRISTMAS

CARRIE LOMAX

CHAPTER 1

❄

NORTHUMBERLAND, 1816

Octavia

Tavi's hands had frozen into claws around the reins an hour ago. Perhaps longer. Time had ceased to have meaning. Her toes were numb, and her nose dripped an endless stream into her woolen scarf.

"Blasted storm," she grumbled to her pony, Nutmeg, who was none too pleased by their predicament, either, judging by her flattened ears.

What should have been an easy half-day ride to her sister's house on a clear, winter morning, had gone disastrously awry. Not far into their journey, the skies darkened. Shortly afterward, gray clouds obscured the sun and icy flakes began swirling in the air.

Despite clear warning signs, Tavi reasoned that it was best to press on. The entire year had been marked by unusually cold weather. There was no telling when the storm might stop. She didn't want to be stranded in an unfamiliar place over Christmas.

Yet somewhere along the way, she'd taken a wrong turn. Perhaps she'd missed an obscured signpost along the road. Or a fork in the road obscured beneath a thick blanket of snow.

She hadn't seen a house in miles. Then again, she could hardly see beyond her horse's ears, pinned back irritably against the wind.

A vicious gust sliced straight through her. The horse shook her mane in protest.

"I know, darling." Tavi patted the animal's neck. The only thing that mattered now was finding shelter before they both froze.

"What's that?" she asked into the arctic air. A bright wink of light in the distance, there and gone. Hope swelled. "A…castle?"

Squinting, she could just make out the dark outline of a building against the snowy gray evening skyline.

"Onward, Nutmeg." Tavi flicked the reins. "Oats ahead. Hay and a nice warm barn. Only a bit farther now."

Or so she prayed, for her stalwart pony's sake.

❄

Ian

IAN TUGGED his scarf higher over the bridge of his nose. His boots crunched audibly as he trudged through knee-high drifts toward the crumbling stable.

Everything at Fellsgrove Castle was a tumbledown, uninhabitable disaster. This glorious mess was his problem now.

"Joyous Christmas tidings, indeed," he groused to no one. He'd asked for this headache. It was only that he hadn't counted on a positively Biblical storm to complicate his "quick" visit to assess the state of his new estate.

The barn door's rusted hinges resisted his effort to pry it open. Ian dug in his heels and pulled, grunting, until it gave way with a groan of protest.

Inside, the air was a few degrees warmer. He tugged wet wool away from his face and stomped the snow from his boots. The lantern he'd left hanging from a post was still lit, the candle flickering as if even fire shivered from the cold. The light it cast didn't reach far, which was why Ian didn't notice the second horse until it moved, startling him.

"What the devil are you doing here?" he demanded. The pony whickered amiably. It was covered in the blanket he was here to place on his own horse, and clearly hungry, for it bent its shaggy head to rattle the empty bucket on the floor. Whoever had put their animal in his sagging barn had helped himself to Ian's oats, too.

To think, he hadn't brought a pistol with him. Why would he, when there was nothing to steal?

After four generations of neglect, there were only a handful of tenants left, none of whom had paid their land rents in decades. All the servants were long gone. Ian needed to rebuild the Susskind dukedom from the ground up.

Until the letter that changed his life, he'd been a simple barrister living an enviably comfortable life in Manchester. He rented bachelor's lodgings from a fastidious landlady, which relieved him of most domestic obligations.

But then Aunt Mag sent him that public notice, and he'd foolishly taken the bait.

You can prove you're the true descendant of the last Duke of Susskind. Do you really want an upstart running off with your rightful legacy?

Why not you? he'd written back.

Four generations ago, the Susskind dukedom had fallen into abeyance. The last living duke had fathered five daughters but no sons, and the letters of patent stipulated that in such circumstance, the women would collectively inherit the title.

In theory, the five sisters could have chosen one amongst themselves to be the heir, but their bitter infighting over their birthright grew to such extremes that even the king declined to intervene, lest he incur the remaining four women's wrath.

Thus began a race to beget the next male heir.

Alas, the Susskind heirs were cursed with a surfeit of females.

Of course, misfortune couldn't last forever. Eventually, a few sons entered the prospective line of succession, but by then, all claims were so attenuated that it would have been difficult to fight off the other claimants. King Charles' declining health precluded royal intervention, and thus the dukedom languished for more than a hundred years.

After four generations, all talk of connections to a dukedom had passed into family lore. The animosity had become so entrenched that no branch of the original family still maintained ties to the rest. Aunt Mags, however, remembered and kept a sharp eye out for any news of potential claimants. She wasn't about to let her great-aunts win.

Pish, Aunt Mags replied. *If I wanted to be a duchess, I'd have applied to Prinny years ago. They would hardly grant it to an old woman, anyway.*

"They" being the Select Committee for Privileges.

Ian felt his mouth tick upward at the corner at the memory. He could practically hear her cackling with glee that her own nephew was to be the new duke, thus ending a century-long feud that had torn the family apart.

A lump formed in his throat. She wasn't here to see it. The old woman had died this past autumn, just weeks before the final decision was handed down.

Damn Solomon Abernathy.

About a year ago, he had submitted a claim to the attorney general, Sir William Garrow, who in turn sent the application to Prince George, at which point his claim was reported in the papers and Aunt Mags read about it. The family being so dispersed and disconnected by this point, a public announcement was deemed sufficient to the task of providing notice to any other potential heirs.

At his aunt's urging, Ian submitted his own petition, at which point Prinny decided he had better things to do than decide the fate of ancient dukedoms and punted the matter to the Select Committee for Privileges.

There, the matter became an elaborate and tedious game of chess. Upon discovering he had competition for his claim, Abernathy filed increasingly strident appeals and generally sought to tie things up in court. Ian strongly suspected he'd won purely because the Select Committee had tired of all the wrangling and chose the less obnoxious petitioner as the heir.

Technically, what sealed his fate was Ian's birthmark. He had been called before the Committee to display his bare bottom, where a reddish spot roughly in the shape of a crown marked his skin, next to the utterly scandalous portrait of his grandfather showing the same mark on his bottom. A similar wine-colored stain was noted in birth of the last living duke, Ian's great-grandfather, thus cementing his claim to the peerage.

Why was there a portrait of his grandfather, naked, in the first place? Well, the man's mistress had been a skilled painter who greatly admired the nude male form. At least Ian had inherited his forebears' enviable physique along with the telltale mark.

Tonight, he would raise a glass to mistresses with a talent for oils.

Enduring the indignity of having his posterior inspected by peers of the realm had been worth the humiliation, though. He'd been formally recognized as the rightful heir barely a week before Christmas, with all the rights, privileges, and complications that came with it.

Such as finding a duchess who wouldn't mind living in a construction site for the next several years.

Difficult to imagine any innocent young lady of superior birth wanting to lodge in this wreck while he pieced it back together, stone by stone.

He gave the pony's nose a final pat, noting the droplets glinting on its mane, indicating a recent arrival.

"Warm up, little one. I don't suppose you can tell me where to find your master?" The animal's ears pricked. He claimed the lantern and ventured forth once more into the frozen world in search of his surprise visitor.

CHAPTER 2

Octavia

Tavi removed her stockings and hung them to dry by the fire, which she'd made out of a broken old chair. She'd pulled its rickety partner close to the grate but hadn't quite summoned the courage to test the seat's sturdiness.

"What is this place?" she wondered out loud, simply to feel less alone. There were signs of life—a kitchen with a bucket of fresh water sitting on the counter, half a loaf of bread wrapped in cloth, and a basket of meat, cheese, dried fruit and eggs placed near the windowsill. Apart from that, this ruin looked like no one had set foot inside for decades. She hadn't ventured far before concluding that this was the best room to rest in.

If only there was a giant stack of firewood next to the imposing mantel. Her pathetic blaze was dwarfed by its ruined magnificence.

One could easily believe ghosts roamed these halls.

Shivering from more than the chill, Tavi clutched her shawl tighter. Despite the fire, she couldn't get warm.

A low groan from the dark hallway she hadn't bothered to explore made her bolt upright.

"Who's there?" she whispered.

Horrifyingly, footsteps echoed toward her.

Tavi grabbed the poker and edged into the corridor. A huge figure like a misshapen man lurched down the flagstones.

She shrieked and lunged.

"What—?"

A man—an actual man, not a phantom out of her apparently fervid imagination—stumbled back. Tavi's aim proved less than accurate. The iron swished harmlessly through the air. He dogged it easily.

"Excuse you," the man said, raising his gloved hands, palms outward, either in a gesture or peace or to strangle her, Tavi wasn't sure. "I didn't expect a woman."

Her fear and ire surged anew.

She was alone in an abandoned building with a stranger who sounded a wee bit too interested in her sex for her comfort, miles away from help. Tavi shrieked and brandished the poker again.

"Don't touch me, you—you scoundrel!"

"Easy, Miss!"

"*Mrs.* Dawson." The lie slipped out easily. She'd used it more than once in her twenty-six years. Spinsters did what they had to do to protect themselves. "My husband went to find help."

"Husband," he echoed, lowering his arms. Tavi raised the poker again. His arms went back up, shielding his face, of which she could hardly see anything, between the edge of his scarf and the brim of his hat. Blue eyes, she thought, but she couldn't be sure.

And what was she doing, pondering the color of his eyes, seconds before he was going to ravish her?

Although, if he meant harm, he wasn't exactly rushing to overpower her. Either he'd been put off by the poker or the mention of her fictitious husband. Or both.

"Where was your husband's mount? I assume that was your pony I found in the barn."

He moved forward. Tavi backed up, still brandishing her weapon.

"Nutmeg."

"Charming."

Was he smiling?

Tavi's heart wouldn't stop pounding long enough for her to decide.

He looked past her, into the room beyond. "Where did you find wood to make a fire?"

"I broke down a chair. It wasn't structurally sound, anyway."

The stranger glanced at her skeptically. "So I understand the situation properly: you put your horse in my tumbledown stable, helped yourself to my oats and a quantity of my hay. Then you came into my castle, broke my furniture and burned it. And now you have the temerity to threaten me with my own fire iron. Do I have that straight?"

Tavi's eyes narrowed. "How do I know you're the owner?"

He laughed. Threw back his head and positively howled. Confused, Tavi's grip on the poker slipped.

"Are you the caretaker?" she demanded. "If so, I'd say your employer has reason to be dissatisfied with your performance. Not a single door was locked, and your sense of hospitality is severely lacking."

"Well, I am rather new to the job," he said amiably. "Why don't you set aside the weapon, Mrs. Dawson. I'll make a pot of tea while we await your husband's arrival."

"He might be some time."

"I imagine so. It's eighteen miles to the nearest town."

"Eighteen miles?" Tavi couldn't conceal her dismay. She'd come twice as far as she meant to, most of it in the wrong direction.

"Worried about your husband?"

"Yes," she snapped. Fine. He'd caught her in a lie, but she wasn't ready to admit it. No sane person would wander off into this storm, and if her husband weren't entirely fictitious, she would undoubtedly be anxious about his safety by now.

"We can go searching for him," the caretaker suggested with a wink in his voice. As if to mock the very idea, the wind howled hard enough to rattle the windows. Miraculously, the ones in this room weren't broken.

Yet.

The wind was trying to change that.

"Mr. Dawson will return when he's ready," Tavi said loftily. The caretaker took hold of her poker. She did not relinquish it. They engaged in an unspoken tug-of-war, each of them not quite yanking hard enough to be rude, but enough to indicate that the other person should relinquish it. Stubbornly, she refused.

He abruptly let go.

Tavi flew backward, dropping the iron with a clatter. Her legs bumped into the chair she'd pulled to the fire, and she sat down—so hard, she crashed right through the seat.

Her cheeks burned as she flailed there, helpless, with her bottom hanging through the frame and her feet too far off the floor to gain leverage.

The caretaker offered her a hand.

Scowling, Tavi took it. He hauled her out and set her on her feet. There was a tear in her skirt, but it could be repaired. She eyed it with dismay.

"Might as well throw another chair on the fire." He turned to her. "Now, Mrs. Dawson, start explaining what you're doing in my castle."

❄

Ian

IAN REGARDED his unexpected visitor with a mix of interest and irritation.

No woman, nor any man, for that matter, had any business wandering around in a blizzard. "Mrs." Dawson was clearly alone, despite her patently false story about a husband who'd gone for help. Had she heard of his recent elevation and come here to seduce him?

A man could hope.

Aunt Mags had warned him—before she died, when it looked increasingly likely that the Select Committee for Privileges would choose his claim—that some women were desperate or unscrupulous enough to attempt entrapping a man. Ian knew this. He simply hadn't considered the possibility in relation to himself until now.

Ian awaited "Mrs." Dawson's explanation for being in his home.

"I was lost and took shelter from the storm in the only place for miles around," she said huffily.

"Don't you mean, *we* were lost?"

"Yes," she snapped. "My husband and I. Together."

"You don't seem very concerned about his wellbeing."

His feisty visitor glared. Her eyes were a pretty shade of hazel, more green than brown. They reminded him of a forest. Enticing, and full of secrets.

Waxing poetic isn't like you. He heard this in Aunt Mag's voice, too.

"He can take care of himself," she said airily, switching from annoyance to breezy unconcern with suspect ease.

"Did he take his horse?" Ian asked, unfastening the toggles on his coat with thawing hands. "Mrs." Dawson wasn't a very good liar, for she flinched visibly. "I ask because I found only one mount in my stable. It's not a large enough animal to carry two people."

"Yes." His visitor scurried to the fire and plucked two lengths of fabric from the mantel, tucking them behind her back. "He took his horse. It's quite likely my husband found another place to stay for the evening."

"Are those your stockings?"

"What? No. Of course not. I would never be so rude as to hang my wet stockings before a fire in a home I'd barged into without permission."

Her lips twitched. So did Ian's. "I see."

"You should feel free to hang your wet clothes to dry, of course. It is your…um…"

"Crumbling castle?" he supplied.

"One can't exactly call it intact."

"No." Ian chuckled bleakly. "It's best described as a ruin."

"I suppose it is." She tugged her shawl around her shoulders. "I must further impose upon your hospitality and inquire whether you might be willing to share some of your supper with me. I found foodstuffs in a basket on the sill over there, and I haven't eaten since this morning when I left home."

Ian was full of questions, but he, too, was starving. They would have to wait for fuller bellies.

He finished divesting himself of his sodden outerwear and turned to find his guest lighting a new candle from the one in his lantern. His breath caught. Her lush figure cast a shadow on the opposite wall. Ian was suddenly warmer than he'd been all day.

She looked up sharply. He averted his gaze so as not to alarm her with the lurid direction of his thoughts.

This would make tonight's sleeping arrangements awkward, indeed.

"I'll see about making supper," he said, stomping into the makeshift kitchen.

CHAPTER 3

Octavia

The caretaker assembled meat and cheese between thick slices of bread, which they toasted over the fire. Warmth slowly crept into her limbs, although her bottom remained cold from sitting on the stone floor, despite three layers of woolen petticoats.

Perhaps she shouldn't have destroyed the only two seats. Even if one was an accident.

"You never told me your name," she said after a comfortable silence.

"Ian Harkness, at your service, Mrs. Dawson."

She didn't regret the lie. Not yet. She was wary of being snowed in with a stranger, even though he'd been perfectly kind to her, in spite of her threatening him with a fire iron.

Tavi sensed regret on the horizon, however. The same way she'd sensed snow today before setting out and believed she could defy nature itself.

She hadn't thought it through before she blurted out that she was married. A wife would naturally worry about her husband's safety in such weather. She kept forgetting to display concern, since he was a figment of her imagination.

She gasped.

Her host tilted his head, watching while Tavi scrambled to her feet.

"The gift!" she exclaimed, wrapping her shawl and cloak around her shoulders, and shoving her feet into her boots.

"What gift?"

"For my sister, Grace. It's vitally important it not be damaged. I spent months making it, and—oh!"

The hinges on the great oaken door creaked as it opened. Icy wind blasted her cheeks.

Mr. Harkness's palm flattened against the wood, to the left of her head. He pressed it closed.

Tavi's pulse raced. Tipping her face up, she studied the harsh angularity of his features. A wide brow adorned with two arching brows to frame those piercing blue eyes. Beneath them, a sharp slash of a nose above sensuous lips.

"Where did you leave it?"

Tavi's mind blanked.

"Leave what?"

"The gift," those lips said, quirking up at one corner. "The one you were so anxious to find a moment ago?"

"In the wagon." Tavi shook herself. What was she doing, staring at his mouth and thinking about how they might feel pressed against hers? "I placed it on the bench, along with my satchel. I didn't want to carry them with me, in case I couldn't find my way inside."

"I'll fetch it." He shoved his feet into his boots and laced them tight, then thrust his arms into his jacket, saying, "I know the grounds better than you do. I'd never forgive myself if you were lost between here and the barn."

"I am not so directionally challenged as to get turned around within sight of a castle!"

Although, her misadventure this morning said otherwise.

Mr. Harkness ignored her protest.

"I'll look for your husband while I'm at it, shall I?" He winked and went out into the dark.

Tavi had the distinct impression he was flirting with her.

She wasn't altogether certain she minded.

❋

Ian

IAN FOUND her battered leather satchel right where she said it would be, tucked beside an unassuming waxed sailcloth bag. He trudged back to the ruined castle with both objects, cursing the wind and missing the warmth of the fire.

His pretty visitor had made herself useful during his absence by washing the few dishes from their supper and putting them away. The relief in her eyes when he returned with her precious parcel twisted something inside him.

"Thank you, I would have been devastated if it were damaged or lost." She hugged the unassuming package.

"Your husband, alas, is still missing." He placed his coat over the edge of the mantel and his boots beside the dying fire. Soon, they would have to go upstairs.

She huffed and rolled her eyes.

"What's in the bag?"

"A gift for my sister."

"Yes, I know that much."

"Baby clothes," she clarified. "Gowns and a blanket and hats and booties and all that. Plus a few new things for her."

"You made all that?"

"I'm an accomplished knitter and an adequate seamstress, I'll have you know."

"Adequate seamstresses are all the rage in London." Catching himself, he added, "Or so I hear."

London was a long distance from Northumberland. A groundsman would have little reason to go there. He didn't wish to reveal his new status quite yet.

She laughed and swatted his arm playfully. Ian's midsection turned warm and slippery inside at the sound.

"How would the caretaker of an ancient pile of barely-habitable rocks know anything which ladies' accomplishments are popular in London?"

Ian sidestepped her question. They were both telling lies, now. He should inform her that this *pile of barely-habitable rocks* had once been the seat of a prominent dukedom, and he'd just been declared the heir.

But his elevation was too new. He still wasn't sure how he felt about being made a duke, albeit a relatively impoverished one. He liked "Mrs." Dawson too much to risk their fragile friendliness by announcing, *I own this property, and, by the way, I'm a duke.* Especially to a woman who was clearly not from the aristocracy herself.

They had that much in common.

What else might he discover?

"Do you and your husband live near here?" he asked.

"Define 'near'."

Ian would define *near* as the way she was standing a little too close to him, toying with the rope like she was about to open it and show him her perfectly adequate accomplishments.

He wished he were that sailcloth bag she was fondling him like the most precious thing in the world.

"In the general vicinity of Beamly," she said, naming what Ian presumed was a village. He had yet to become familiar with the area, beyond riding through towns on his way here.

Tavi tipped her auburn head, considering. Her hair caught the light like living fire. Ian had to tamp down impulse to run his fingers it. To pull her to him and taste her lips…

But that would cause all kinds of problems.

"About ten miles from here. I've heard of an old castle that once belonged to the Duke of Susskind, but the line died out. I never expected to set foot inside. Fellsgrove, I think it was called." She looks about the dark room. "That's what this place is, isn't it? The old duke's country seat?"

"Indeed, you are correct, Mrs. Dawson."

"It's been abandoned for a hundred years," she said wistfully. "Imagine, letting such a grand property as this fall into disrepair. Some say it had so many windows that the tax burden exceeded the rents, so he pulled through roof off."

The truth was more mundane than the story local residents had concocted: poor management of finances and disinterest in maintaining the property had led the last duke to abandon it in favor of more comfortable and cosmopolitan lodgings.

"In fact, I've never heard of there being a caretaker." Tavi shot him a wary glare. "You don't seem old. Or terribly established."

Ian chuckled. "I am a recent arrival." Taking a rusted pan, he nudged the glowing embers into it and gestured to the lantern. "If you don't mind carrying that, I'll show you upstairs to the sleeping chamber."

His guest stiffened. Her chin dipped. There was nowhere to sleep on this level, and not enough firewood to keep the room warm, either.

"This way," he said, leading her into a dark passageway.

As if this situation could get any more awkward…

CHAPTER 4

❄

Octavia

Tavi eyed the small chamber warily. Specifically, the bed.

Part of her longed to climb beneath that cozy-looking down coverlet. Her feet had re-frozen during the brief climb up the dark stairwell. But it wasn't hers to claim.

"It's only for one night." She sighed. A white cloud billowed into the air.

"Unless this keeps up."

To emphasize Mr. Harkness' point, wind howled outside the boarded-up windows. The old-fashioned four-poster had been pushed near the hearth, where the caretaker knelt to build a fire from the remnants of the one downstairs, tossing logs onto the grate to make a crackling blaze.

They both studiously ignored the bed. It didn't look large enough for two people. She would have to sleep practically on top of him. Or he on top of her. If they were to share it.

Oh, dear. Where was her imagination going?

Tavi had learned the hard way never to trust handsome, charming men.

She liked Mr. Harkness. Too much. She barely knew him.

It had been years since she'd been young and foolish enough to let a man touch her, a decision that resulted in such shame that she'd sworn never to give into temptation again.

But the fact that they would never meet again made the idea almost irresistible.

Her mother had taught her that all a woman needed to do was glance in a man's direction and he would desire her. They were weak creatures, easily tempted, like Adam with Eve. In Tavi's experience, their interest extended only as far as the bedroom—not all the way to the altar.

But couldn't women be tempted, too?

That's what she felt, looking at him. A fluttery sensation in her belly. Heightened awareness of her own skin. Not quite nervous, but alert to his every movement. Her gaze kept coming to rest on his face. Each time she pulled it away, reminding herself not to stare, then found herself studying his features again.

"Will your husband be troubled by his wife sharing a room with another man for an evening, Mrs. Dawson?"

She really needed to drop the fiction that she was married. Tavi licked her lips.

"No." Changing the subject, she asked, "Is there a place to wash up for the evening?"

"In here."

Mr. Harkness rose fluidly and led her to a small antechamber. He leaned past her to press the door open with his palm flat to the wood, just as he'd done before when he spared her the cold trek to the barn. Tavi caught the faint scent of freshly cut wood and a hint of smoke. She liked it. Wanted to rub herself in it until—

Enough with that foolishness.

In the antechamber, the frigid air was a bracing reminder that she could not afford to be tempted by him.

"You'll want this." Mr. Harkness offered her the lantern.

She took it and made use of her tooth powder, soap, and hand towel, helping herself to the bucket of fresh water. Rough lodgings, but far better than freezing to death in a hedgerow.

"I've never seen such cold weather," she said briskly, returning to the chamber with the single bed. "Not in all my twenty-six years."

"The Thames froze over a few years ago." He'd returned to sitting by the fire. "Believe it was 1811 or 1812."

Beside him sat a thin blanket and a small bundle that could make a poor excuse for a pillow. She frowned at that. Dimly, she recalled reading about the river, but Tavi was distracted by the makeshift bedroll.

"You don't mean to sleep on the floor tonight, do you, Mr. Harkness? You'll freeze."

"I hadn't noticed an alternative option being available. In fact, I can confirm that the only bed is the one I brought with me."

"The entire thing?"

"Not the frame. I found that in the storeroom, disassembled. The ropes were rotten, so I used planks to support the mattress. Everything else I brought with me, Mrs. Dawson, for I believe rest cures all ills."

"You won't sleep well on the floor."

"No."

He turned so his face was in profile. A tense beat of silence passed.

"We could share—" she started.

"I'll flip you for it," he said before she could finish that sentence. Embarrassed heat crawled over her skin. He held up a coin. "Heads or tails?"

"Tails," she blurted. Tavi always chose tails, for it sounded closer to her pet name.

"Heads I take the floor, tails, you take the bed."

The coin glinted, spinning in the air.

"Wait! That isn't fair!"

"What do you know, I lose." Mr. Harkness feigned sadness.

"You're teasing me," she grumbled.

"I haven't begun teasing you, Mrs. Dawson."

"It's Tavi. My given name is Octavia, but everyone calls me Tavi. Please, Mr. Harkness, I'd appreciate it if you did the same."

"My name is Ian. I prefer it to Mr. Harkness, which makes me sound like I'm a clerk or a barrister or something terribly stuffy like that." He laid out the blanket on the stone before the fire and placed the bundle where his head would go. "Now lay down. I won't allow a lady to sleep on the floor."

Obediently, Tavi crawled beneath the coverlet. Mr. Harkness—Ian, rather—took his turn in the makeshift privy and returned to the foot of the bed, where he sat.

"How late do you think it is?"

"Not very. Seven-thirty, perhaps eight."

"No wonder I'm not tired."

She was, in a physical sense. Riding on horseback for hours had her muscles stiff and sore. Tomorrow would be worse.

"I'm not either." He leaned against the foot of the bed. Wood creaked. "Tell me, what takes you to your sister's two days before Christmas, Tavi?"

"She's just had a baby."

"How recently?"

"Yesterday. I would have gone sooner, but the baby came a bit earlier than we expected."

Tired of speaking to the back of his head, Tavi turned herself around so her feet were by the pillows and her arms crossed at the foot of the bed.

"As often happens. Do you like babies, Mrs. Dawson?"

"I love them. They're so adorable and helpless. How can anyone not enjoy babies?"

"They're smelly and they fuss, and they keep godawful hours. The cute stage only lasts for a short while before they become proper children, and then it's pure mayhem."

"Do you speak from experience, Ian?" she asked with bated breath. Perhaps he was married. Deflating thought.

"Lord, no. I can't be trusted with a child." He chuckled. "I have no siblings, but I have several friends who insist upon producing as many children with their wives as the ladies will allow. Absolutely ruins them as drinking partners."

Tavi swatted his shoulder, laughing. His response caused a knot inside her to loosen.

She couldn't remember the last time she'd had fun with a man this way. At one of the festivals held in town, although a spinster being too familiar with men made tongues wag, so she usually danced a few reels before going home to her ailing mother. Ordinarily, she was wary of the opposite sex, but Ian had moved right past her defenses.

Or, perhaps, she was keen to capitalize upon an opportunity to spend time with a charming man without anyone knowing.

Admitting it to herself cost her pride nothing.

"Can I interest you in a warming taste of whisky?" he asked.

Tavi hesitated. "I have no head for the stuff."

She hadn't ever tried a drink stronger than cider. Her face was warm from proximity to the fire. She sat up, dangling her stockinged toes over the foot of the bed. The pillows were too far away for the heat to penetrate.

"I'm afraid I've only the one glass. We'll have to share."

He poured two fingers of amber liquid, followed by a generous splash of water.

"Doesn't that ruin it?" she asked.

Ian shook his head. "It opens up the flavor. Try it."

A frisson skittered along her spine when their fingertips brushed. He had nice hands. Big enough that the glass looked tiny in his grasp. Tavi cradled it, sniffing.

"It smells like heather," she said. "With a hint of lavender and an undertone of peat."

He smiled. Her heart gave a startled thump.

"You're already a connoisseur, Mrs. Dawson."

She wrinkled her nose and raised the glass to her lips. The scent was stronger up close. Her first sip seared straight down her sternum. Holding the drink out so as not to spill it, she thumped her chest.

"Burns, doesn't it?"

He shifted and took it back, offering her water from his canteen. She drank deeply. Her head already felt fuzzy.

"I don't feel the need to try that again," she declared, settling back down on her stomach with her head near his.

"More for me." He sipped. "It helps if you go slowly."

"Let me try again."

He passed it over without commenting on her abrupt change of heart. Their fingertips brushed again. An electric jolt shot down her midsection when their gazes clashed and held.

If she leaned forward, their lips would meet.

"We could share it," she blurted out. "The bed, I mean. Like we're sharing this."

She tipped up the glass and drained it to cover her embarrassment.

CHAPTER 5

❄

Ian

Twin bright red roses bloomed on Tavi's cheeks—and once the majority of his whisky went down her lovely throat, that flush crawled down her skin and disappeared into the high neck of her nightgown.

His cock twitched against the confines of his trousers. He shifted position in an attempt to conceal his reaction. Ian had a fair sense that if she knew he wanted to roll her onto her back and rip that modest garment right off her splendid body, she would run out into the blizzard without her boots.

She clearly didn't know what a temptation she was.

As befitted an honorable new duke, Ian resolved to ignore his baser impulses. He would not take advantage of a woman who had no choice but to shelter with him. As much as he didn't relish the prospect of sleeping on a cold stone floor with nothing but a thin wool blanket and his rolled jacket for a pillow, he didn't trust his gallantry to last until morning if he took Tavi up on her offer.

Not with the way she was looking at him.

"I don't think that's a good idea," he said, gently.

Tavi's blush retreated instantly. She dropped her gaze and pushed back to sit on her heels in the center of the small bed.

"I didn't mean anything by it," she said, clearly flustered.

Ian tipped back the last of the whisky into his mouth and got up, feeling his willpower crumbling, like stones falling from his castle walls.

"I feel terrible for putting you out of your own bed. I should be the one to suffer by sleeping on the floor, for being so stupid as to ride through snowstorm and get lost." She rolled off the side and popped up to standing. The top of her head barely came to his chin. He could just imagine how perfectly her breasts would fit in his hands—

And that was exactly why he shouldn't get in with her.

Even if it was cold.

No matter how his cock ached for her.

For all he knew, Tavi was a virgin spinster. Or genuinely married, and her husband for whatever reason allowed his wife to wander off in dangerous weather.

A man that careless with his wife doesn't deserve her.

"You've endured enough punishment for one day, Tavi."

Ian splashed more whisky into the glass. The last drink had been more water than spirits. This one was not. He savored the way it burned all the way down, dampening his lust.

Momentarily.

"Besides, we discussed this. I'm not taking the bed," he added.

With her fists on her hips, the woman glared at him. Ian crossed his arms over his chest. The quelling effect of the alcohol wore off the instant her gaze flicked admiringly down his torso. Then upward again. She mimicked his stance.

"Well, I'm not taking it, either."

With a swirl of auburn hair and white nightgown, she plopped herself down in his makeshift bedroll. She even made it so far as to pull the scratchy blanket over her shoulders and turn to face the fire. Stubborn woman.

"Get up, Tavi."

"No."

He blew out a sigh.

She'd attacked first. He was only retaliating.

Ian scooped her into his arms. Tavi, startled, yelped and latched onto his neck like she was afraid he'd drop her from a great height.

She felt too good pressed against his chest to do that.

"You're not playing fair, Harkness."

"You're not abiding by our agreement, Mrs. Dawson."

She rolled her eyes. "You cheated."

It was on the tip of his tongue to retort, *you lied*. Instead, he dropped her onto the soft bed. Tavi squeaked. Her hair fanned out. Raking it away from her face, she knee-walked to him, fisted his shirt, and dragged him down. Ian fell with a grunt.

"See? We both fit. Now go to sleep."

She threw the blanket over his half-prone form. Ian's legs stuck out of the down coverlet.

Sleep. Yes, that was a totally reasonable order.

He tucked his legs under the covers. If he kept his trousers on, he should be able to conceal his raging erection beneath layers upon layers of fabric. It's warmer in the bed, his stupid heart insisted. Only his brain thought this was setting himself up for disaster, and it was addled with the excellent whisky he'd bought himself to celebrate his newfound status.

Which she didn't know about.

Tavi liked him enough to share a bed with him. He liked her enough to share everything but the truth of who he was.

"What would your husband say, Mrs. Dawson?" he drawled, yawning.

Beside him, Tavi stiffened.

Oh, shit. Was she married, after all?

❉

Octavia

THIS WAS the time to admit she'd lied. But even though Tavi had recklessly decided to share the tiny bed with him, she wasn't sure how he would react to sleeping beside her. She wouldn't mind kissing him, but beyond that?

Her body might say yes, but her good sense held her back. *You're being a fool*, she told herself. *He hasn't offered a kiss. Or anything else.*

She burrowed into the down-filled coverlet, taking up as little space as possible while Ian rearranged himself on the mattress. They lay there, side-by-side, touching as little as possible, for several breathless moments.

"Ian?"

"Yes, Mrs. Dawson?"

"I'm about to fall out. May I move closer?"

He grunted and shifted slightly. Tavi wriggled until their shoulders touched. Her foot brushed his leg.

"Ian?"

"Yes?"

"I'm not married."

He chuckled, a low rumble that did more to warm her than a blazing bonfire would have. "I guessed as much. Why are you telling me the truth now?"

Her cheeks warmed. *Because I want to kiss you.* "I don't like lying."

"Does anyone?"

"There are people who don't… never mind."

He didn't press the point.

"Any woman who's frightened enough to attack a man with a poker can be forgiven for creating a fictional husband for protection. I didn't intend to scare you, earlier."

Mortified, Tavi pulled the coverlet up to her chin. "I was ridiculous. Breaking into an empty house and then coming at you like that."

"It's forgotten. If I may ask an intrusive question, how did you wind up a spinster?"

Tavi made a face. "Poor luck and a poorer attitude, if you ask my mother. You can't, though, she's deceased."

"I'm so sorry."

"Don't be. It was a relief, in the end. She was very ill, for years."

"And that's why you never married?"

"Partly. I did have a suitor once. We planned to marry."

"Why didn't you?"

"He'd promised the same to another woman."

"Rude."

"Terribly. She had a dowry three times the size of mine and didn't have an ailing mother to care for. The news of his wedding came as a complete shock."

"This is cold comfort, Tavi, but I'm glad you didn't end up with him."

"I am, too." She sighed. "After that, I focused on caring for my mother. I never really found time to seek a husband." Tavi stared up at the ceiling. "It's not as if I had many callers. My choices were few and far between, what with this hair."

The mattress dipped as her companion shifted. Tavi's heart thumped against her ribs. She shouldn't have said all that. She'd always had a habit of being too open, too honest…*too much.*

Ian propped himself up on one elbow, looking down at her.

"I think your hair is beautiful, Tavi." A small smile tucked the corner of his mouth, popping a dimple. "I hope your former intended is pleased with his bargain, because he certainly lost out when he didn't choose you."

Tears burned Tavi's eyes. No one ever told her she was beautiful. No one looked at her with desire the way Ian was now. She couldn't imagine walking away from him tomorrow morning without trying.

Twining one hand up behind his neck, she pulled him down and pressed her lips to his.

CHAPTER 6

Ian

Tavi was one Christmas indulgence Ian couldn't afford. Which meant he shouldn't let this go on one single second longer.

And yet, he couldn't stop. She tasted of warm whisky and willing woman, and Ian couldn't remember the last time he'd felt more than a fleeting connection with…anyone, come to think of it.

Gently, he broke the kiss. He couldn't resist cupping her face as he said, "I meant it when I said your virtue was safe with me."

"What virtue?" Tavi tucked a strand of hair behind her ear. The apples of her cheeks flushed charmingly, visible even in the low light. Ian wasn't so drunk on whisky and the heady touch of a woman that he missed the flicker of shame over her expression. "My betrothed and I anticipated our wedding vows on a few occasions."

Inwardly, he groaned. Anticipation surged.

"Why tell me?"

"I feel I can trust you with the truth. After all, the chances that we'll meet again after tonight are slim."

There was no mistaking the sadness in her voice. She had no

expectations of him—which was usually how Ian preferred his assignations.

Not this one.

He liked Tavi, what little he'd seen of her. Their attraction was unmistakable.

As a duke, he would be expected to marry into the aristocracy, a class he'd had little occasion to interact with until very recently. His bride would likely be a shy virgin. Ladylike ignorance might appeal to men who relied upon it to conceal the fact that they were selfish in bed, but the thought left Ian cold. To him, there was nothing appealing about the prospect of fumbling around trying to figure out how a woman wanted to be touched while she lay there like a dead fish.

Ian shuddered at the thought. He preferred a woman who knew what she wanted. Like Tavi.

"You can trust me," he murmured. "Should our paths cross—and I hope one day they do, Mrs. Dawson"—she swatted his arm, laughing—"I won't whisper a single syllable to anyone about what transpired here tonight."

"Good, for my sister has—" Tavi bit off. "Never mind. Shall we continue this?"

She stretched up to kiss his jaw. Ian dared to brush his thumb along the underside of her breast over the wool of her gown. She arched into his touch, so he rolled her nipple beneath the pad of his thumb.

"Tavi."

"Mmm?"

"You're wearing too many clothes."

"I am rather warm." She grinned, flashing even white teeth between kiss-swollen lips. "Warmer than I have been all day, in fact."

Ian just grinned and hiked up the hem of her gown. She helped him, stripping the woolen garment over her head with a staticky crackle and tossing it on the floor.

Tavi laid with her head propped on one hand, the dying fire illuminating her lush hips, in a nigh-transparent chemise. His mouth went dry. He knew she had a mouthwatering shape, but her nipples, barely visible through the thin lawn, sent a shudder of need coursing through him.

Tavi tossed her auburn hair over her shoulder. "Mr. Harkness, have you considered making yourself more comfortable?"

"Come to think of it, I am blazing hot."

Had woolen trousers ever taken this long to unfasten and kick away? He tugged off his shirt and the layer beneath, too, leaving him in his visibly tented smallclothes.

Tavi's gaze flicked to them, then back to his face. She brought her hand to his chin and stroked her thumb along his lower lip.

"I propose we take no risks tonight."

Ian swallowed. He hadn't expected a beautiful woman to warm his bed—literally—this evening. He therefore had no right to disappointment.

Her hand moved down. "No permanent entanglements." A surge of lust made his cock twitch. She kissed him and carefully palmed him. Exploratory. Gentle. "Apart from that limitation, I propose we enjoy our stolen holiday together."

Ian took her hand and pressed it firmly to his cock. "I accept your proposal, Mrs. Dawson."

She laughed, rolling her eyes.

"I'll never live down the way I phrased that, will I?"

"The joke will be forgotten by Christmas."

There was a flash of sadness in her beautiful eyes, replaced with anticipation when he leaned forward, pressing her into the bedclothes, and kissed her deeply. She opened eagerly to the sweep of his tongue. Ian settled himself between her glorious thighs and exhaled against her temple.

Her chemise was still too much of a barrier between their skin. For the moment, he contented himself with squeezing the globe of her breast. Tavi arched into his touch with a soft moan.

That sound unraveled him. Inhibitions melted like ice tossed on a fire—with a hiss, as he tilted his hips to bring his cock into closer contact with her center. He tugged the hem of her shift higher. They both went still when his palm landed on her bare skin.

Tavi twined her arms around his neck. The heat between their bodies was enough to make the cold air on his back a thrill. She nodded once.

"We'll stop before this goes too far." A promise Ian wasn't sure he could keep if Tavi changed her mind again. She'd let down her guard gradually throughout the evening. Watching her thaw had been a pleasure in its own right.

He found her breast and squeezed again, drinking in her moan. Tavi required little encouragement to abandon her shift entirely, raising her arms and letting him peel it over her raised arms. When it was where it belonged—on the floor—he set about feasting on her, sucking the nipple deep into his mouth while she clutched his hair and made delicious, needy sounds.

When he'd had enough of one side, he switched to the other, giving it the same treatment. Ian felt his good intentions crumbling with each wriggle and scrape of her nails across his nape.

He explored the dip of her waist and the slight rise of her belly, with its perfect indentation of a navel decorated with a few scattered freckles. Her perfection could not be adequately explored without the application of his tongue. Tavi squirmed.

"Hold still," he ordered, and she tried. She honestly did. He could tell from the way her lower lip caught between her teeth and the dark pools of her eyes when he slid his hand to the cleft at her center.

"Is this too far, Tavi?"

Her autumn-hued hair fanned out across the pillow as she shook her head and breathed, "Keep going."

Ian watched her reaction as he dipped one finger inside her. The bite on her lip deepened. Her delicate chin tipped upward. So did her hips. He slowly pumped in and out, testing her. Finding what she liked best. His cock kicked against the mattress in futile protest at this delay.

Your services won't be needed this evening, he warned the part of him trying to hijack his self-control.

Bending his head, he pressed his tongue to the soft pink slit and licked. Tavi made a strangled sound.

"Still alright, Mrs. Dawson?"

She huffed. "I've never…"

He grinned. "Never had a man lick your quim?"

A glimpse of her face revealed cherry-red cheeks and a flush that went all the way down to her chest.

"You like it when I do this, don't you?" He demonstrated, then returned to pumping two fingers into her, watching her response. "Wicked girl. You want me to spread you wide and fuck you with my fingers while I lick you into oblivion, don't you?"

She barely managed a nod. Her knees fell wider as she scooched toward him in wordless plea.

"So responsive. Such a good lady, aren't you?" He gave her a light lick, just a tease. She grabbed his hair and gently tried to hold him in place while raising her hips, but that made him lose the rhythm with his fingers. Ian adjusted and said, "Hold still, Tavi. I'll give you everything you need if you tell me what you want."

"Your mouth," she said instantly. Ian's lazy gaze skimmed down her body, trailing scorch marks along her abdomen.

"Where do you want it?"

"On me. On my—er, quim."

Ian grinned with satisfaction. "Very good, Tavi."

He bent his head and went to work.

CHAPTER 7

Octavia

Tavi fisted the sheet with one hand and clutched Ian's hair like it was the only thing anchoring her.

He licked a long stroke up her center, circled the tip of his tongue around the sensitive nub at her core, and flicked it with steadily increasing pressure while curling his fingers to hit *exactly—that—spot…*

Her thighs and back tensed all at once as the first wave ripped through her body, bringing her off the bed to witness the obscene view of Ian's head between her legs and his knowing blue eyes looking right at her.

An unladylike wail clawed its way out of her throat. Tavi gasped, suspended in a paroxysm of pleasure that wouldn't stop. Breathless. He didn't stop. He kept going until she collapsed onto the pillow, panting.

Ian crawled up to join her with a smug look on his face.

"Don't you look satisfied," he said, kissing her. There was a hint of herself on his lips, but Tavi didn't mind. She rather liked it.

"You don't," she said, though he did, in the way of a man who knew he'd done his job thoroughly and well. His cock twitched insistently against her belly. Needy. Demanding. Ian pulled her on top of him and kissed her tenderly.

"We only take this as far as you want to go," he reminded her.

Tavi edged her way down his body, exploring him the way he'd done with her. She kept having to pause and tuck her long hair behind her ears. Ian gathered it in his big hands and held it aside, a courtesy she found unexpectedly arousing.

She paused to admire the breadth of his shoulders and the planes of muscle on his chest. Below that were his ribs, which proved to be ticklish when she found the right spot. He tensed.

"Quit poking me," he grumbled, covering his flanks. Contritely, Tavi moved on. She traced her way down his defined abdomen. His fabric-covered cock kicked when she settled her breasts over it, the better to examine his stomach.

"I can take these off," she said, propping her chin on her hand and toying with the knotted drawstring. The ruddy head poked between white linen and his skin. Tavi traced the pad of her thumb in circle over the weeping slit.

"Careful, Tavi."

"Only to do what you did for me. If you'd like that."

He covered his face with both hands and groaned.

"Take them off."

She took her time obeying. With slow, delicate movements, such as one might use when approaching a frightened animal, she untied the string and edged the fabric down until his cock sprang jauntily free.

I've certainly set myself up for a challenge, haven't I?

Her mouth watered. With a quick glance at Ian, she took his shaft in hand, squeezing lightly. Testing. Those muscles on his stomach contracted distractingly. She didn't have muscle there—or if she did, what existed was covered in a layer of softness. There was nothing soft about this man. Even his teasing humor held a sharp edge.

Tavi touched her tongue to the rude, round tip and watched him react. His eyes half-closed, yet more intense than ever before. She shivered. Not from the cold.

He gathered her hair loosely and held it aside, like drawing the curtain of a performance he couldn't tear his gaze from.

She applied herself as best she knew how, having only done this on one other occasion. She hadn't enjoyed the experience then, but this was different. They were strangers. Nothing to one another. Tavi didn't have to worry that one disappointment would stain their relationship forever.

Freeing, in a way. This could go horribly sideways and she'd only have to face the embarrassment of one awkward morning.

She therefore took him so far into her mouth that she thought she'd choke. Her jaw ached as she met each thrust of his hips. Wet sounds that should disgust her, but didn't, echoed in her ears. She kept her attention focused on his stomach. The ripple of muscles was her barometer of how much he was enjoying this. That, and his groans, a low counterpoint to the sucking noises she was making.

Experimentally, she squeezed the orbs at the base of his cock. He shuddered, so she did it again, pleased with his reaction. It was different from when she'd poked him in the ribs. That had been a moment of humor to break the tension. Touching him this intimately heightened it.

Part of her wanted to slide up, open her legs and impale herself upon him. Yet a few moments of dubious pleasure—she had never gotten much out of her erstwhile suitor's ineffectual efforts—would lead to weeks of anxiety until nature confirmed she hadn't ended up in her sister's situation: pregnant and unmarried.

Tavi shook away the intrusive thought. She wasn't going to let that happen to herself, and she trusted Ian not to put her in that position, either. They barely knew one another, but he'd been rakishly honorable since the first moment of their acquaintance.

"You don't know what that does to me," he groaned. Tavi rolled the base of his cock again, then set herself upon him, hollowing out her cheeks as she took him as deeply as she could.

Remembering how much she'd liked it when he looked up at her, she kept her gaze fastened on his face, cataloging his expressions. Memorizing them for later, so she could return to this evening long after they'd parted ways, when she spent lonely nights in her bed at the cottage.

He especially liked it when she stroked her thumb along the underside of his cock. She did it again, firmer, and exulted in his response.

"Fuck," he said through gritted teeth. His grip on her hair tightened, pulling at the roots. He held her there, hips bucking up while she tried to take as much of him as she could. Each time she thought she'd found her limit, a tug on her hair made her relax just enough to take him deeper. He swelled between her lips. Impossibly hard. An impossible texture against her lips. Soft skin over thick veins. Heat. So much heat and friction…

Tavi couldn't maintain eye contact. She let her lids flutter closed and gave in to his instruction, trusting him to guide her. Bliss.

A choked sound brought her back to reality.

"Tavi, I—"

She tasted salt. His grip loosened, giving her the opportunity to escape before he crested. She gripped the base of his cock and stroked the way he liked, sucking hard. A hot pulse hit the back of her throat. Tavi made herself relax and let her throat work, taking the second wave. Then a third. Only when his stomach smoothed abruptly and his breathing evened out did she finally, reluctantly, release him.

"Oh my god," he murmured, staring up at the ceiling with one arm flung over his half-closed eyes. "You've ruined me for all other women."

Tavi laughed, exultant as she crawled up the mattress to tuck herself into the crook of his arm. He smelled like salt and fresh-cut wood. His skin was feverish despite the cold. "You're ridiculous. I'm sure you say that to all the women who…do that."

"Believe it or not, I don't make a habit of playing the Corinthian." He yawned and dropped his arm around her shoulders, tugging her close.

Tavi wriggled out of his grasp, wincing when her bare feet hit the stone floor.

"Where are you going?"

"To get my shift. In case I need to get up during the night, I don't want to have to go searching for it in the darkness."

For no rational reason, Tavi felt that sleeping naked with him was more intimate than pleasuring one another. She wasn't quite ready to take that step.

Gratefully she crawled back into his warm embrace. Heat enveloped her, radiating off his skin. Soothing. Ian dropped a lazy kiss on her forehead and said, "Sleep well, Mrs. Dawson."

Tavi grinned. Outside, the wind howled.

CHAPTER 8

❄

Octavia

Tavi awoke slowly, baffled by the weight slung across her waist and the wall of heat at her back. The tip of her nose was cold, so she burrowed into the warmth…and felt a sizable lump beneath her bottom.

Ian Harkness.

Abandoned castle.

Last night.

Tavi's eyes flew open. Wan light crept in around the boarded-up windows. The wind had barely diminished its banshee shrieking. Clearly she must wait a few more hours before setting out.

Guilt pricked her conscience.

Poor Grace. All alone on Christmas Eve with a newborn to care for.

Yet her sister's circumstances would not improve if Tavi took Nutmeg into a snowstorm and got lost again. She therefore snuggled into Ian's warm arms and fell back asleep.

❄

THE SECOND TIME she awoke within the safety of Ian's arms, Tavi found him watching her. What could have been strange instead felt comforting.

"Good morning."

"Thought you were going to sleep until noon."

"What time is it?"

"Around eight. My pocket watch is on the chair. I checked it a little while ago when you starfished me out of bed."

Tavi poked him in the ribs. He flinched, chuckling.

"I do not sleep like a sea creature."

"Do so. You make a beautiful star, too."

Ian pressed her into the pillow with a lingering kiss.

Her heart melted. She couldn't have conjured a more perfect man than Ian Harkness. How cruel of fate to send her the man of her dreams and then give her a single night with him.

If she was only to have this one time, Tavi wanted to experience it to the fullest. She knew how to mitigate the risks.

In theory.

She was the one who told Grace it wasn't so terrible to anticipate your wedding vows, as long as you were careful about it. After all, she'd done it and come away with no one the wiser.

But Grace hadn't been as lucky. Or, perhaps she and Solomon hadn't been quite as careful.

Tavi would exercise caution, though. Once shouldn't pose a great risk.

"Ian."

"Hm?"

"I changed my mind."

He went still. His cock was rampant against her thigh. He shifted restlessly against her. Tavi skimmed her hand down his naked arse, finding an odd bump on the left buttock. She traced the shape absently. It reminded her of a crown.

"About?"

"Would you promise not to finish inside me?"

Ian kissed her temple. "I would do anything you asked for the privilege of being inside you, Octavia Dawson."

She brought her hands up the broad planes of his back. Ian kissed his way down her body the way he'd done last night. Her nipples peaked into hard points. He closed his teeth around one. Tavi gasped and arched into his mouth. He soothed it with a gentle lick, then moved to the other side.

He nipped her inner thigh. She yelped. The sting faded into a pleasant warmth.

"That's retaliation for taking up the whole bed," he informed her. "Now be a good girl and open for me." Banked heat came into his eyes. He draped her leg over his back. "That's it. You'll come for me this way, and then again on my cock. Right?"

Tavi managed to nod, her hair scratching on the pillow case. She was already so wet and ready for him. He didn't need to do this, but she greatly enjoyed his efforts and wasn't inclined to stop him.

This time, he took his time teasing her. Keeping her right on the edge. No matter how much she squirmed and sighed, or tugged his hair, he refused to give her satisfaction.

"Ian," she demanded. "Stop tormenting me."

He grinned wickedly. A shocking thrill coursed through her at the sight of his chin dripping with evidence of her lust.

"You want to come, Tavi? Say it. Beg for it. Then I'll make you come so hard you see stars."

Words erupted from her mouth in a needy, breathless chant. "Please, Ian. I'm begging you. Let me come. I need this. I need you to—"

He bore down on the aching nub at the apex of her sex and crooked his fingers. Tavi's thighs locked. Her heel dug into his back. Her fingers clutched blindly at his hair.

She saw stars.

Galaxies of them.

Tavi collapsed into the sheets, boneless and panting. When she could breathe again, Ian had crawled up to her, full of smug satisfaction. "I adore this look on you." She kissed him.

"What look?" he asked innocently.

"Like you've won a competition for an unfathomably huge prize, and you're basking in your success."

A shadow flickered over his face, too fleeting for Tavi to parse.

"I have," he said. "Your pleasure is a prize worth winning." Ian settled himself between her thighs. "Now, are you ready to come again?"

"Not yet. I need a minute."

"Let me help you get there," he said, slicking his cock along her center. Tavi gasped. She felt so empty and aching. She tipped her hips up. He sank in an inch, but held back. She whimpered protest.

"You want me to fuck you, Tavi?"

"*Please*."

He thrust forward, filling her so suddenly and completely that she had to sink her nails into his shoulders to stay grounded. Already, the pressure coiled in her belly. He withdrew and sank deeper, groaning against her temple.

"You feel so good, Tavi. So tight and hot. Aching for me."

"Yes," she managed. He set a relentless pace. She locked her legs behind his waist.

"I've ached for you, too," he declared through gritted teeth. "Ever since you threatened me with a fire iron, I wanted you. Your tits in my hands. In my mouth. I could hardly sleep last night. I couldn't stop thinking about sinking my fingers into your hips and watching your arse bounce as I took you from behind."

"Let's do that," she gasped. "I want you in me that way."

Ian withdrew, leaving her with an empty ache. Tavi got onto all fours. He gripped her hips and slid into her from behind, penetrating even deeper. Harder than she thought she could handle, until after a few thrusts she arched her back and discovered she loved him pounding into her this way.

Tavi reached between her legs and stroked herself.

"Good," he growled. "Touch yourself while I fuck you, Tavi. Come for me. Come hard on my cock."

She obeyed. The climax tore through her. Wrenching. Blinding. She whimpered when he withdrew as the last waves of pleasure coursed through her body, leaving her with her face pressed into the pillow and her bottom high in the air.

His harsh gasp preceded the first streak of hot liquid that hit her back. Startled, Tavi managed to peer over her shoulder. Ian stroked himself fiercely, his expression twisted in a grimace bordering on pain as fluid shot from his cock onto her back. It dripped down her sides. Some of it puddled between her shoulder blades.

Tavi simply let it happen, fascinated and slightly appalled that she could find this enjoyable, yet she did. She loved what he was doing. Ian had remembered to withdraw. She'd expected it to be awkward and embarrassing. He'd made it the opposite.

"I've made a complete mess of you," he said with a hint of chagrin.

"Indeed." Tavi didn't know whether she should get up, or what to do. She'd never been in this position before. Literally.

"Wait here."

"I have nowhere to go," she said, though it wasn't entirely true. She did need to leave. The problem was that she wanted to stay here in a crumbling, abandoned castle, and keep doing this with Ian.

Tavi sighed. Ian returned with a damp cloth.

"I'm sorry it's so cold," he said.

"Everything is cold," she said, wincing when he gently stroked her back to clean her up.

"I could have heated water first."

"I'd rather not lay here with…you know. You dripping off me."

The rims of his ears turned red. "There is quite a lot of it."

They took turns washing in the makeshift privy. Ian went downstairs while Tavi dressed. When she came down, she found breakfast ready for her.

"What's this?" he asked while she was fussing with a small branch of pine that still had needles.

"I'm making a tree."

"That's not a tree, it's a yew branch."

Tavi glared. "I can see that, Harkness. Would you have me send you out into the snow to cut down a fresh one?"

He snagged her around the waist and kissed her.

"I'd do it if you asked me to."

Tavi giggled. Flutters in her stomach. How was she supposed to leave him?

She must, though. Grace was all alone with a newborn and no one to help her. Tavi hoped to convince her to come stay at the cottage, but in her letters, Grace insisted she wanted to remain in Newcastle upon Tyne to wait for Solomon's return.

Last night had been a wonderful interlude that she would treasure forever, but making a clean break was the best path forward for both of them.

"I can imagine this room with a roaring fire and an enormous tree, decorated with glass ornaments and candles," she said wistfully. In the daylight, the castle's rough-hewn charm shone through the time-wrought destruction.

"You have a better imagination than I do, Tavi."

She tipped her head, pondering the edge in his voice.

"Shall we go and ready your horse?" he asked, shrugging into his coat.

Tavi hastened to put on her boots and collect her belongings.

CHAPTER 9

Ian

Ian watched Tavi and Nutmeg ride off into the bleakly beautiful landscape with a pang of regret.

He shouldn't have let her go.

Yet he had no rational reason to detain her—and several important reasons to want her gone. He'd lied to her, if only by omission.

Her sister needed her more than he did.

Ian wanted her to stay, but he didn't need her the way Grace did, and he certainly wasn't in a position to begin a romantic entanglement. He had nobles to impress. Even if Tavi had professed a love of this ruin and spoke longingly about seeing it restored, that didn't mean she wanted to be its mistress.

He could hardly ask a woman he barely knew to navigate the pressures of a dukedom with him, when he didn't know the first thing about how to be a duke, himself.

Whether or not she would make a good duchess, he knew with certainty to the marrow of his bones she would make an excellent wife and mother. He was utterly baffled why any man would choose to marry for money when he could wake up to Octavia Dawson in his bed every morning.

Men were, as a general category, fools.

Ian set about rolling up the mattress. He didn't want to leave it until his next visit, lest mice turn it into a nest. He needed to hire a land steward and an agent, once he gained access to the accounts associated with the dukedom. With most of the people who decided his fate away for another fortnight, that would mean another few weeks' delay. Until then, his elevation was mostly an abstraction.

The bedding and pillows went into a sack, but not until after he'd held them to his nose to inhale the lingering scent of Tavi's hair.

He cleaned the makeshift kitchen, packing away the extra food and baskets. The very last thing he did was put out the fire.

Beside it sat the "tree" Tavi had set up, complete with its sad red ribbons from her stocking. Ian's mouth quirked up at the corner, even though it made his heart sink just a little bit more.

Out into the blinding bright world. He slitted his eyes against the sun and snow and trudged through the drifts, nearly bent double by the heavy sack on his back.

When he made it to the barn, his vision took almost a full minute to adjust. Ian tossed the rolled mattress into the wagon and missed. It bounced off the wall and thudded to the ground. He cursed. On his second try, the thick roll landed in the flat bed. Springs squeaked. A horse whickered.

"You'll be hauling this all the way back to Manchester," he advised Cinnamon, his chestnut gelding. "Best buck up. It'll be a long, cold haul."

Thirty minutes later he had the horse hitched to the wagon, his ruin of a home locked and boarded—to what point, he didn't know; there was nothing to steal—and was about to mount up when he spotted a smallish package sitting near the door and froze.

"Shit."

Tavi's gift.

He couldn't let a baby and a new mother go without the clothes Tavi so carefully crafted for them. Not at Christmas.

His heart gave a thump.

Yes, he was a duke. But a desire to keep his uncomfortable secret was no reason not to make a little Christmas delivery of his own. She'd mentioned her sister lived in Newcastle upon Tyne.

A grin split Ian's face as he smacked his horse into a trot. Drifting snowflakes stung his cheek. He whistled a merry tune into the brisk air.

❄

Tavi

Tavi paid to put Nutmeg in the crowded public stable some distance away from Grace's rented flat. From there, she trudged through the dirty slush-covered streets. The address wasn't a slum, but this row of listing multistory buildings wasn't far above a slum, either.

She found the uninspiring doorway to her sister's lodgings, an address she had memorized from their frequent exchange of letters, but never visited in person.

"Ick." Tavi juggled her satchel so she could hold her skirts out of the melted snow on the stairs. The smell of overcooked cabbage permeated the air. A noisy family lived on the first floor, with children shouting and pots banging.

"How is Grace managing these steps?" she huffed a few minutes later, to no one in particular. At the second landing, she stopped to rest. A thin wail echoed down from above.

"I'm coming, little one." Tavi hoisted her luggage and stomped up to the top floor. "I have a nice gift for you," she huffed. At the top was a door with a barely-visible number marked on its surface.

It took Grace forever to let her in. Tavi took one look at her sister's red-rimmed eyes and the tiny bundle in her arms and dropped her things beside the door.

"How can I help?"

Grace burst into tears.

"I can't believe he left me here all alone," she sobbed. "And I haven't anything to cook for Christmas dinner. I haven't been able to manage the stairs and I can't leave this one alone to go to the market..." Graced bounced the fussing baby.

"Everything is going to be alright," Tavi said firmly. She sent her sister back to bed with orders to nurse. Despite her aching toes, she went back down all those steps to the market where she was able to buy a pullet for a bargain price, along with potatoes, a cabbage, and onions. It wasn't much, but for two people, it would suffice.

All the time, her ire at Grace's absent fiancé grew.

What kind of man abandoned his pregnant bride-to-be? At Christmas, no less?

Surely Solomon Abernathy had meant to be here for the birth of his son. Mr. Abernathy never struck her as a reliable sort, but Grace loved him and felt certain he was set to rise in the world. Something about a dukedom that had fallen into abeyance. It sounded far-fetched, but it *was* possible. Unlikely, but possible.

Back upstairs, with her basket from the market Tavi put the chicken on to roast with the potatoes and then went back down to fetch water. She put a kettle on to heat and went to check on her sister.

Grace sat on the edge of her bed, utterly exhausted.

"Would you like me to take him?" Tavi asked.

"Please."

Tavi accepted the infant, marveling at his smallness. Only three days old, his head was still squished into a cone from the birthing process. "You're a sweet boy, aren't you?" To her sister, she asked, "What's his name?"

"I haven't decided yet. Christopher, perhaps, after Father? Or Noel. In honor of the season." She yawned. The poor woman probably hadn't slept since her son's arrival, which was no good for either of them.

"Noel is a wonderful name."

Tavi took her nephew into the other room and washed him, changing his nappy and re-wrapping him in the makeshift swaddle. This would be a good time to give Grace the gift, but her sister had fallen asleep. Her stomach rumbled as the scent of roasted chicken filled the air.

The baby slept in a basket near the fire while she set the table, singing a Cornish song:

The first Nowell, the angels did say/was to certain poor shepherds in fields where they lay/In fields, where they, lay keeping their sheep…

This flat was grim and Grace's prospects worse, but Tavi meant to help her sister in every way possible. If her mind wandered to Ian and the time they'd shared at Fellsgrove—more often than she'd like—then it was her secret to hold close to her heart.

When she heard Grace stirring in the bedroom, Tavi took her a pitcher of warm water to wash with.

Tavi went to her satchel and opened it. Her stomach sank through the floor. Tears burned her eyes.

She'd lost it.

All that work, for naught.

Grace and Noel's Christmas gift was gone.

CHAPTER 10

Ian

Ian tried three stables before he found one that had space for his gelding and the wagon. It took an hour of inquiries before he Grace Dawson's unassuming residence.

He mounted the stairs with trepidation.

There were a lot of very steep stairs. How recently had her baby been born? He thought Tavi had said quite recently.

At the top landing, he hesitated.

A baby's wail steeled his resolve.

Ian knocked. He waited with bated breath.

A woman with hair like Tavi's, and similar features, opened the door.

"Do I know you?"

"I'm looking for Octavia Dawson."

She frowned. "Wait a moment." The door slammed shut. Feminine voices carried through the thin barrier.

Ian's pulse thundered in his temples. He startled when the unoiled hinges screamed.

"What are you doing here?" Tavi demanded. Her eyes were red-rimmed as if she'd been crying. The scent of baked chicken hit his nose. Ian's stomach gurgled.

"You left something." He held up her gift. Tavi gasped, clasping her hands over her heart.

"You found it! You brought it! I was devastated to think I'd lost her gift!"

Grace observed all of this somberly. She still appeared to be pregnant. Ian understood that to be normal for women who'd recently given birth. He hoped she hadn't been forced to do so alone, in this uninspiring lodging house.

Tavi clutched the bundle, her eyes shining. She motioned for him to come inside. Ian's boots thumped on the bare wood floor. There were only two rooms, a bedroom and a main living area. Beside the stove was a nearly-empty box of coal. Above it hung a sprig of pine, tied with a frayed ribbon. He smiled at Tavi's attempt at festivity. The place needed a dose of cheer.

"This is my sister, Grace," she said distractedly, indicating the woman who had answered the door, who was now bouncing a fussy newborn.

"A pleasure. I take it this is your new arrival?"

Grace shot her sister an unreadable glance. "I named him Noel. Since his father isn't here to have a say in the matter."

"A pity. Is your husband not returning for the holidays?"

"I'm not married."

Ian winced. Tavi never mentioned that detail.

"Solomon suffered a setback recently and decided he needed to seek his fortune abroad. He paid the rent on this palace"— she cast a scathing glare around the hovel— "through the end of the month, and booked passage to the Indies."

"Ah."

Excellent response, there, Ian chided himself. Mysteriously, his easy-going charm had abruptly deserted him, leaving Ian with clammy palms and a prickling sensation crawling over his skin. He hadn't felt this nervous since baring his posterior before the Select Committee for Privileges—and even then, he'd been more irritated than anxious.

"Won't you introduce your visitor, Tavi?"

"I am Ian Harkness."

The pleats in Grace Dawson's brow deepened, but she said nothing. Tavi bustled around the table, setting out a skimpy chicken and roasted vegetables, with a fresh-baked rolls that smelled absolutely divine. Ian's stomach rumbled. Loudly.

"And how do you know Tavi?" Grace asked suspiciously.

"I met Miss Dawson when she was forced to shelter at Fellsgrove Castle last night. During our visit, she impressed upon me how much time she had spent making this gift for you and your new arrival, so when I discovered she had left it behind, I decided to bring it to her. It took me a bit of time to track down where you lived—"

"You went to a great deal of bother."

"Grace." Tavi gasped. "Surely we can at least be polite, after he's gone to so much trouble for us." She cast him a rueful glance.

"Apologies, sir," Grace said without contrition. "I am not fit company right now."

"It's perfectly alright, Miss Dawson. I interrupted your dinner."

He was imposing. He should go.

Tavi turned away from the stove, dusting her hands on her apron. "Please. Join us." She grabbed a chipped plate from the shelf and set it between the other two. "It is the least we can do to thank you."

Grace didn't want him there. He should decline the invitation.

Tavi tucked a strand of hair behind her ear. At least he wasn't the only nervous party. He hadn't thought about how coming here revealed that his feelings were more than mere kindness.

"Where are you staying tonight?" Grace asked.

Ian turned questioningly to Tavi, who didn't meet his eye while she removed a steaming pot from the stove and placed it on the sideboard.

"I haven't thought about it yet. An inn, assuming I can find one."

There was an awkward silence, until the baby's fussing turned into a screech.

"If you'll excuse me," Grace said, going to the bedroom and shutting the listing door with a slam.

"I am so sorry about her inhospitable attitude this evening. She's overwhelmed, you know, with Solomon going off like that. He told her it would be better if they married when he returned, but honestly, I don't think he has any intention…" She broke off. Worry clouded her beautiful eyes.

It dawned on Ian why Grace might have recognized his name. His recent social elevation had been publicly recorded in the press from London to Edinburgh. He shifted uneasily.

Solomon Abernathy was the name of his rival for the dukedom. If he'd led Grace on with the idea of making her a duchess, then abandoned her to seek his fortune in India…

Ian shuddered at the implications. But he was not going to be the second man to abandon the Dawson women. Not at Christmas. He couldn't answer for Abernathy's actions, but he could help them, once he had access to all the rights and privileges due to him.

Except, he'd never mentioned that pesky detail about his dukedom to Tavi.

That did make the situation rather sticky.

"Please, sit. We'll be ready in a few minutes."

"How can I help?"

Unable to think of another solution, Ian busied himself helping prepare for their evening meal. Together, he and Tavi bustled around, setting out the fresh-baked rolls and side dishes of potatoes and cabbage. Not a fancy meal, by any stretch, but a filling one.

For two.

"Wait. I have something to share, too." From his rucksack, Ian produced the rest of the cheese, cured meats, butter and jam.

When she saw it, Tavi made a noise of protest.

With a quick glance at the closed bedroom door, he brought his hand up and stroked his thumb along her cheek. "I can't in good conscience take food from a new mother on Christmas, Tavi. This is barely enough for two women, never mind a man with a healthy appetite. Let me contribute."

"But I am already in your debt," she protested. "Several times over. I cannot tell you how much I appreciate you bringing Grace's gift all this way, Ian."

He was on the verge of kissing her, or inviting her to stay at an inn with him—or both, if only he could untangle his thoughts enough to say it out loud—when Grace and Noel reappeared with a grouchy slam. Tavi whirled away.

Perhaps Grace's attitude would improve if she had a few moments to herself. If she was willing to relinquish her son for a few moments.

"May I hold him?" Ian asked, reaching for the baby. Grace reluctantly surrendered her son. It had been a long time since he'd held an infant. He was taken off-guard by the surge of need that swamped him as he inhaled the child's briny sour milk scent. Tiny fingers curled around his thumb.

When he could tear his gaze away from Noel's unfocused blue eyes, it went immediately to Tavi.

He wanted her at his side.

He wanted her for his duchess.

Most of all, he wanted babies. Their babies. Together.

The thought sent heat rushing through his blood. He loved Tavi. His head was spinning from how quickly it had happened, but he wasn't going to let her walk out of his life—or ride away—a second time.

He shifted on the three-legged stool, holding himself as straight as if it were a throne.

Grace can't stay here.

He wasn't going to say it out loud, but the uncomfortable truth loomed over their paltry meal. She was weeks away from being able to manage those stairs. She'd be out of a home in a week, anyway, unless she had money saved to pay another month's rent.

He was a duke. That meant he had to help Tavi's family, even if she didn't know about his title yet. In a couple of weeks' time, he would be comparatively wealthy. Not by duke standards, perhaps, but definitely by theirs.

Tavi wouldn't need to spend her savings on jewels and fine dresses. She was the *perfect* duchess for a dukedom that needed to be rebuilt from the ground up.

"Have you sorted out where you'll sleep tonight, Mr. Harkness?" Grace asked. Her demeanor had grown progressively friendlier as her belly had filled. Hunger had a way of sharpening one's temper. Sitting back in her chair, she sighed. "It's late. If you need to stay here, Mr. Harkness, you may. We have no bed, however."

"I might have a solution for that. If I won't be too much of a bother."

Grace nodded, and yawned.

Ian strode out into the night, lugging his mattress roll and bedding up the stairs. When he came back, Grace and the baby had retired to the second room for the evening.

He and Tavi pushed the table near the window to make space for his pallet on the floor near the stove.

"This looks cozy," Tavi said, her shawl falling down around her elbows. She twisted the ends and let them unfurl, over and over, a mindless exercise he recognized as the product of anxious nerves.

"There's only one question left," Ian said, a sly note creeping into his tone. "Where will you sleep? With your sister…or with me?"

A blush stole over her cheeks.

"We can't do what we did last night," she said.

"Or this morning?" he teased.

Red-faced, Tavi smacked his chest.

CHAPTER 11

Octavia

Tavi awoke to sunlight streaming in through the window and a baby's contented gurgle. She stretched, then belatedly wondered where Ian had gone.

Twisting, she found him standing near the window holding Noel. Her heart thumped.

His disheveled hair stuck up every which way. A scruff of unshaven beard darkened his chin. His eyes were soft as he patted the baby's back.

Her breath caught. She'd never seen any man as beautiful as he. Ian would make a wonderful father. He was patient and gentle, with an airy sense of humor that made even the darkest conditions feel brighter.

If she hadn't already been halfway in love with him, the sight of Ian holding a baby sent her tumbling right over the cliff.

"Morning," she said, scrambling out of the pallet.

"You're awake. If you'll take a turn holding this little one, I'll put water on for tea."

Last night had been a test of temptation. They made it through without engaging in too much untoward conduct. Furtive kisses. His hand beneath her nightgown. Nothing more, for Grace's sake.

They had standards. Besides, it was rude to flaunt their happiness before a woman devastated by abandonment.

"Yes, we do, don't we?" she crooned to the baby. He was wrapped in the swaddle she'd embroidered for him. The stitching was a little crooked in places.

"Admiring your perfectly adequate handiwork?" Ian teased. Tavi laughed. The bedroom door creaked open, startling them both. Grace emerged, somber, holding a letter.

"It's you, isn't it?" she said somberly. "You're *that* Ian Harkness. The new Duke of Susskind."

Tavi laughed. "Are you sure you're not feverish, Grace? What an absurd thing to say."

"He didn't tell you, did he?" Her sister's dark eyes cut to hers. "Mr. Harkness isn't the caretaker of Fellsgrove, like you assumed. He was just recognized as its rightful heir. It was announced a few weeks ago. Right before Solomon left England."

Tavi felt her jaw drop. That couldn't be right.

Turning to him, she read the truth in the guilt written on his face and felt like she'd been plunged into a cold bath. Dropped into a snowdrift. An unpleasant shock to the system.

If he was a duke, that changed *everything.*

He'd been toying with her. She had no reason to expect anything from him—that wasn't part of their bargain—but his unexpected appearance had made Tavi hope their one night could lead to more.

"She's mistaken. Isn't she?"

Noel fussed. Ian passed the baby to his mother, who bounced him absently. Ian poured the steaming kettle over a tea pot and set it aside as if the thing was made of glass instead of iron.

"Your sister is correct."

Tavi felt dizzy.

Five minutes ago, she'd been entertaining a wild fantasy of being his wife and bearing his children.

What a joke. Dukes didn't marry country spinsters. When it

came to handsome men, she had less sense than your average goose—and worse luck.

"Please leave, Mr. Harkness." Grace choked. Tears brimmed in her eyes. "If not for you, I would have a husband right now. Solomon promised he would make me a duchess." A choked sob burst out of her. "He abandoned us because of you. I want you to go."

Grace clutched son to her chest and slammed the door to her room. Her sob shattered Tavi's heart into pieces. How could have she betrayed her sister so profoundly? So unwittingly?

She was a fool.

"Tavi, please, I—"

"Go, Ian," she said woodenly. She slipped into Grace's bedroom and leaned against the door, listening to him pack up his belongings. It didn't take long.

Outside, church bells pealed.

❄

Ian

He should have told her. This whole situation was his fault. A lie by omissions was no less painful than a falsehood.

If only she'd let him explain.

Ian threw the bundle of his bedding into the wagon with more force than necessary. The cold stung his cheeks. The world shouldn't be this bright. It should be swirling with angry storm clouds to match the bitterness in his heart.

Not once had he ever considered being rejected by a woman for becoming a duke. He'd imagined every possible outcome, but that one.

Octavia Dawson surprised him at every turn.

Ian's heart fell through his stomach, battering each rib on the way down like a stone thrown into a chasm.

"Let's go," he told Cinnamon. They trotted into the yard. He would be best served by returning to Fellsgrove for the night rather than trying to find an inn along the way back to Manchester. But his castle would be forever haunted by Tavi's ghost. He couldn't bear the thought of returning there.

The horse's tail flicked as they trotted out of the stable yard.

Imagine. He and his rival for the Susskind dukedom had both managed to fall for one of the Dawson sisters.

Coincidence didn't begin to describe it.

What a scandal. Once word got out—and it would, quickly—he'd be utterly disgraced. Not to mention that business with his birthmark and the scandalous painting, which was bad enough.

Ian's mouth ticked up beneath his wool scarf. The situation would be darkly amusing if it were happening to anyone else.

Since it was happening to him, his smile faded as quickly as it came.

Heartbreak was pure misery. No wonder he'd spent so much of his life avoiding it. Wasn't until Tavi came at him with an iron poker that he let his guard down enough to fall for a woman…

Which meant that he had a choice.

He could turn tail and run away. Accept rejection and take the blame for events beyond his control. It wasn't his fault that he'd been born with a hereditary birthmark on his bottom. He'd only heard the name Solomon Abernathy in court documents.

Or he could be like Aunt Mags and refuse to let history shape his future.

No.

Ian wasn't leaving yet. Grace had thrown him out of her house in a fit of temper, but Tavi would listen if he got her alone. He was going to fix this mess.

Ian had no intention of extending the family quarrel into another generation. Grace might be justifiably angry with him, but Tavi didn't deserve her sister's ire.

Determined, he turned his horse down a narrow street, whereupon he found two petite women standing outside arguing about which direction to go. One carried a baby-shaped bundle.

The other was Tavi. Her auburn hair flowed down her back, gleaming in the bright winter sun.

Ian hauled back on the reins. The wagon juddered to a stop.

Before he knew what he was doing, Ian leaped out. Startled, both women looked up. Grace frowned. Tavi's pretty eyes flared wide.

"No, Tavi, I'm not leaving you," he declared, storming up to the women. "I am not as craven as Solomon Abernathy. I would never be the kind of man who abandons his wife and child. Furthermore, I'd have gladly provided him with a living, if I'd known about the situation. It was never mentioned in the court documents, nor did he reach out to me directly. He could have done, if he wanted to."

"He'd have been too proud to accept." Grace sniffed. She looked worn and tired. "When his claim to the dukedom was denied, he decided he would make his fortune elsewhere. I didn't want to believe it, but now I can accept the truth. He wishes to keep his marital options open in case a richer bride comes along."

She sniffed. That had been Ian's impression of Abernathy as well, but he didn't have the heart to say it. Like Tavi, Grace had learned the hard way not to take men at their word.

He could give them a reason to.

"How about we make him rue his greed?" He winked. Grace eyed him warily.

He took Tavi by the shoulders. "This will cause a scandal, but I am asking you to marry me."

"Me? A duchess? You must be joking."

"Not remotely, darling. I know we've only just met, but this tiresome peerage has caused more family strife than any title could ever possibly warrant. First in my family, now in yours. I say we resolve the conflict through our union. I shall settle a generous amount upon Grace, which should enable her to find a husband. If she chooses Abernathy, I can try to use my newfound influence to have him elevated to a peerage, even if it's only a baronetcy."

"He wouldn't deserve it," Grace said flatly.

"But you do."

For the first time of their acquaintance, she gave him a genuine, if wobbly, smile.

"We hardly know one another," Tavi said slowly, as if she were tempted but didn't quite trust him enough to say yes.

"Then let's spend the next fortnight together. I have no close family to celebrate the holiday with, and no pressing business to attend to until after Twelfth Night. If you're willing, I could join you and your sister." Ian gave a lopsided grin, fully aware that baring his heart didn't mean she would agree to his abrupt proposal.

"I—well—if it's alright with you, Grace—"

"Yes! Tavi, I would never want my woes to deprive you of your happiness. I haven't been very welcoming, but I hope you will forgive me in light of my circumstances." She nudged Tavi. "Besides, while it's a bit crowded, your beau is in possession of a wagon. Nutmeg can't carry us both."

"I would be delighted to drive you away from this place, Miss Dawson." He turned to Tavi. "It's settled, then."

Startled hazel eyes met his. Her lips parted. Before she could utter a word, Ian bent to claim them in a fierce kiss. She didn't resist. Tavi melted against him. Ian hadn't expected that, either. His arms slid around her back, pulling her closer. Deepening the kiss.

"Ahem."

Reluctantly, Ian pulled back. Tavi's cheeks were bright red. Shyly, she tucked a strand of hair behind her ear.

"Your lordship—" Grace said.

"Who?" Ian cast about. "Oh, right. Me."

A reluctant smile tugged at Grace's lips. He'd come so close to making her laugh. "I'm just Ian. No matter how many titles they grant me."

He earned a chuckle for that.

"Ian, then. I feel terrible about what I said this morning. Your name seemed so familiar. It bothered me all night. This morning, I went through Sol's letters. It was quite a shock to realize that you were the same man he blamed for stealing his birthright." Grace sniffed. "Upon reflection, I don't believe his claim to the title was ever as solid as he led me to believe."

Ian could have told her as much. More importantly, the Select Committee for Privileges had agreed. Solomon's branch of the Susskind family tree was so far removed from the main line that it quickly became clear he was relying on sheer ambition and disinterest from the other prospective heirs to win the title.

A fact that did nothing to soothe Grace's wounded heart. She heaved a sigh. "In retrospect, the reason he didn't marry me right away when I fell pregnant was that he believed he would inherit the dukedom and wed an heiress instead. He thought I would be content to be his mistress," she said indignantly. "And when he didn't get his way, he left."

Yes, that all dovetailed with what Ian had seen of Solomon Abernathy. Covetous, shallow, and entitled.

"I am so sorry, Grace. You deserve so much better than that." He brushed a fingertip along the baby's plump cheeks. Noel gave a fluttery sigh. "So do you."

"I admit I was jealous for a moment," Grace said with a sidelong glance at Tavi. "It felt like my sister had everything I wanted. But she was as aghast as I was. I know Tavi would never have intentionally betrayed me…and that opened my eyes to the true culprit." She placed a gloved hand on his forearm. "I don't wish to ruin anything for you. Please don't let me stand in the way of your happiness."

"This is all my fault," Ian said. "I should have told you my true identity from the first moment we met."

"You mean when I was brandishing a fire iron at your head?"

"You did *not*, Tavi!" Grace gasped.

Ian chuckled. "After you calmed down. The truth is, I never sought a dukedom. My aunt insisted it was rightfully mine if I bothered to claim it. But why would I want to deal with politics and nobles who are bound to hate me for my inferior upbringing?"

"The money attached to the estate wasn't an inducement?" Tavi teased.

"There isn't as much money as you might think, and most of it will be allocated to rebuilding Fellsgrove." He shrugged. "I was comfortable in my bachelor existence. Until I met you. I realized I didn't want to become a duke all alone."

Ian caught Tavi around the waist and lifted her into the air. She squealed, her skirt belling out, until he dragged her close to his chest and set her upon the ground.

"Shall we go and celebrate Christmas properly, darling?"

CHAPTER 12

❄

Octavia

If she'd known Ian was a duke before she'd met him, she would never have had the courage to kiss him.

Or make love to him.

Or attack him with a poker, for that matter.

It was for the best that he'd kept that secret from her. At least at first. Once the initial shock passed, she forgave him wholly and completely.

Her heart was so full as they drove up the road to her mother's cottage—now hers and Grace's—that she couldn't help but look into the sky and feel a surge of gratitude for vicious snowstorms and forgotten gifts.

"This is quaint," Ian said. "Charming."

"It's where we grew up." She reached over to squeeze Grace's hand. "Our parents raised ten children in this cottage. There will be more than enough space for the four of us."

It was truly a Christmas miracle how easily everything had been resolved.

Ian needed a place to stay near Fellsgrove while he oversaw the restoration and expansion of the ancient ducal seat. He'd already given Tavi a signet so large it slipped off her thumb. She was wearing it on a ribbon tied around her neck until he could get her a proper betrothal ring.

The idea of being a duchess felt very distant. She leaned her cheek on Ian's shoulder. He dropped a kiss on the top of her head. They would figure it out. Together.

Inside, Tavi lit a fire in the central grate while Grace settled into the chamber on the main floor. Ian tended to Nutmeg and Cinnamon. By the time she had a blaze roaring and was beginning to wonder what was taking so long, he returned, stamping his feet and carrying a huge armload of yew branches.

"It's not a tree, but this should serve for now, right?" He winked. Tavi laughed in delight. Together, they hung the boughs, tied bows on them, and lit candles in glass jars. Together, they stepped back to admire their handiwork. "One day, I'm going to give you a proper Christmas tree at Fellsgrove Castle. Just like Queen Anne at Queen's Lodge, Windsor. Once restored, it would be the perfect setting for a rustic tradition."

"I'll hold you to that promise," Tavi said. "We'll hold a ball for all your fancy new friends. Assuming anyone will deign to acknowledge a duke married to a commoner."

"But see, that is why I need you, Mrs. Dawson." She swatted his arm, laughing. "To keep me from getting an inflated sense of my own self-importance as I rise in the world. You'll keep me grounded."

He dropped a kiss on her cheek. Her insides turned slippery and warm. She could hardly believe her good fortune. Her mother had always said, *when you meet the right man, you'll know*. For years, Tavi believed she'd squandered her chance at love.

As it turned out, she needed to get lost in a storm to find the right man for her.

While they'd only been acquainted for a few days, Ian slipped into her life as if he'd always been a part of it.

Later that evening, Tavi led him to her bedroom. Compared to the rough conditions of the castle, it was a palace. Still, it was hardly suitable for a duke. Ian didn't appear to mind. Their clothes fell to the floor amidst a flurry of more kisses. This time, there was no question of who would take the bed. They both would.

Tavi fell to her knees and stroked his cock, running her thumb along the underside the way he liked. Ian's gaze turned intense. She squeezed her breast, offering it. Showing it off while she swirled her tongue over the tip. He groaned and tightened his grip on her hair.

"You've a wicked tongue, love, and you put it to good use."

He dragged her up for a kiss. Ian dropped onto the edge of the bed, hooked his arm behind her knee and pulled her into his lap.

"I want you this way," he declared roughly. "Your tits in my face while you ride my cock."

Tavi squirmed. "And you say I have a wicked tongue, when you're the one who says such filthy things."

"You love it."

She sank down on him in response. "It feels like I was missing a part of myself before I met you," she whispered. "You complete me. Fill me so full I'm overflowing."

"I haven't, but I fully intend to, darling." His hot gaze ranged from her breasts to her face, then back down. "This time, I'm not pulling out."

"Good," she said fiercely. "But you'd damn well better marry me before we have babies."

He guided her hips up and down, setting a fast pace, racing to the finish. "I promise. I'm going to give you the biggest, gaudiest ring anyone ever beheld. An enormous ruby as red as your hair, with diamonds. Anyone who sees it will know you're my wife, Tavi. My duchess. Our children will have lives such as we can only imagine."

"Yes," she hissed. "I want all of that. With you."

He bent his head and sucked the column of her throat, grinding down. Tavi's world contracted until he was the only thing in it. Hot fluid flooded her. Her entire body tightened as if trying to hold him inside her.

"God, yes, Tavi. I love the way you come on my cock. I love you."

Exhaling, he buried his face in the crook of her neck. "You are, without a doubt, the very best Christmas gift a man could ask for." He pressed a gentle kiss to her throat and rolled them back onto the mattress. "A beautiful wife to remind me of my roots. No matter how high we climb in society, we'll do it together."

EPILOGUE

❄

FIVE YEARS LATER - CHRISTMAS 1821

Octavia

Tavi teetered on the tippy-top of a tall ladder.

"A little to the left, my lady."

She gritted her teeth and stretched out her arm. She was never going to get used to being called *my lady* or *your grace*. She'd long since decided to treat it as a grand joke. "Duchess" was a role she playacted on occasion with her nice new friends.

Some of the aristocrats weren't so nice. She'd learned to ignore them.

The gold ornament listed slightly to one side, but Tavi managed to get it in place. Perfectly adequate placement, if she did say so herself.

"Octavia Harkness Susskind!"

Startled, she lost her grip on the ladder. Her heavy emerald velvet skirts pulled her off-balance. "Oh—ohhh—OH!"

Tavi toppled into her husband's arms, laughing.

Ian wasn't quite as amused.

"I told you we should have chosen a smaller tree," he grumbled.

Twining her arms around his neck, she dragged him in for a kiss. "I was in no danger. You caught me."

"Minx."

Gently, he placed her on the ground.

The footmen who'd been assisting her by holding the ladder and calling out the placement of ornaments, had discreetly scattered after removing the offending device.

"Me, me, me!"

Startled, they turned to find their infant son crawling as fast as he could, giggling wildly, with a stuffed toy in the shape of a cat clutched in one tiny fist. Their toddler daughter chased after him, enraged at the theft of her favorite toy.

Tavi exchanged a bemused glance with Ian. They divided to conquer, sweeping in to rescue their children before they escalated into outright war.

Ian corralled his kicking, screaming little girl, Mimi. Her nickname came from the way she screamed *me* instead of *mine* whenever her brother made off with one of her toys. At two-and-a-half, her vocabulary remained an adorable work in progress.

Tavi cocked her hip and wrested the disgusting object from her son's drooling mouth. Deprived of his stolen prize, he kicked and wailed.

"No, darling. That's your sister's kitten."

He launched into an enraged squall.

"Did you get around to making him one?" Ian, the Duke of Susskind, patted Mimi's red curls and tucked the soggy, misshapen stuffed animal into his daughter's arms. She quieted instantly, putting the plush beneath her chin with her thumb held sullenly between plump red lips.

"Still trying to finish it." Tavi kissed her son's head before handing him to their nurse, who arrived belatedly at the scene of the crime. She handed him off to Nurse, saying, "This one needs a bath."

"He shall have one, Your Grace."

Inwardly, Tavi winced. She had no patience for this fashion of high-born ladies handing their children over to paid minders— but she had guests to prepare for, and to be honest, she didn't mind having help. As inconvenient as they were, she and Ian preferred to have their children underfoot. It kept life interesting.

It felt like family.

Still, a duchess had a certain image to uphold—and even if hers was hardly the most elegant or fashionable, Tavi had cultivated a circle of friends who appreciated her warmth and lack of artifice. The ladies helped her navigate the unfamiliar, and often unspoken, rituals of the peerage, while their husbands helped Ian forge connections. With Fellsgrove mostly restored, he was becoming an influential politician.

He could have married a highborn lady. To Tavi, it spoke well of his character that he'd been aware that he could turn into a pompous bore and chosen to marry her before the peerage rearranged his entire life. They'd managed the ensuing scandal, and the transition, hand-in-hand.

"This one needs a wash, too." Ian set Mimi on the floor. She refused to release him until her Da walked her to Nanny and told her she must go up for her bath, now.

Even then, Tavi and Ian still weren't alone. Amazingly, despite the restoration and expansion of Fellsgrove Castle, Tavi constantly found herself tripping over maids and footmen. They were everywhere, lurking about, trying to be helpful at every turn.

Tonight, she needed to get her husband alone. Truly alone. Her gift for him was not meant for public view.

She grinned just thinking of it.

"Ian."

"Darling?"

Tavi went to her oversized Christmas tree and tugged a box about the size of a Bible out from under it. She felt her husband's palm slide down the curve of her bottom while she was bent over.

"Cheeky devil."

"You love it."

"Speaking of cheeks, open this. I made it specially for you." Tavi glanced around. Spying two footmen and a maid, she clapped her hands loudly. "Leave us."

When they were *finally* alone, Ian tugged the ribbon and removed the lid. Tavi bounced on the balls of her feet.

The box fell. Ian examined her painting with an expression of shock that quickly transformed into peals of laughter.

"Five years of lessons, and this is your choice of subject?"

"It's a perfectly adequate painting!"

"More than adequate, darling. But why on earth did you choose to show me posed naked on a divan?"

"To commemorate your birthmark." Tavi giggled and slid her hand down his ass, squeezing where the red spot appeared on his left cheek. "Without that fortuitous quirk of physiology, we might never have met. Besides, you never know when one of our descendants might need to prove his parentage!"

She winked. Ian roared with laughter.

"Shall we hang it in the gallery?" He studied the picture as though it were, indeed, fine art. Ian had managed to track down and purchase the portraits of many of his ancestors, yet the nude of his father remained sadly out of reach, being the property of his sire's mistress' grandson, who was unwilling to sell it. For the moment. He and Ian had developed a cordial relationship over a series of letters — one of many family branches he had managed to repair ties with.

"If it were larger, I'd say we should hang it above the fireplace for all to admire," he added, holding it up.

Tavi couldn't suppress her chortle. "Wouldn't that impress Lady Umbridge."

The marchioness had turned up her nose at them and led many of the *ton* to follow her example. Being snubbed stung at first, but Tavi had expected some degree of rebuke for, as some women phrased it, *getting her hooks into him before better-bred ladies had a chance.*

"Maybe we should let Grace decide where to put it."

Tavi smacked Ian's arm. "My sister does not need to see your naked posterior."

"You painted it."

True enough. Hanging it in the gallery was, of course, out of the question. They needed to find a way to get it out of sight, lest their guests be affronted. Tavi wasn't worried about Ian being embarrassed. She had long since learned that he was nigh unembarrassable.

Hence, her gift.

"Speaking of Grace, when do the Emersons arrive?" he asked, sliding the painting back into its box for the time being.

"Soon. Any time now." Not long after being jilted, Grace met a widower, Mr. Emerson. He had a daughter a few years older than Noel, whom he treated as his own son. Seeing their children play together was one of the highlights of every Christmas.

"Remember when we first sat before this fireplace?" Tavi said wistfully.

"You mean the night you sat in a chair and fell through the seat, so we burned it?"

She swatted him, laughing. Ian sobered and said, "I remember every moment of that night, Tavi. I remember thinking I had never met such a beautiful, brave woman. I thought, if anyone could help me get through the challenges of the next few years, it's her. And you have."

Tavi couldn't breathe. Couldn't swallow past the lump in her throat.

"Every day, I am so glad I met you, Tavi. I hope we're here every Christmas for decades to come. I hope our children find delight in decorating a tree beside this ancient fireplace, and their children, and their children's children. I never want to see our family torn apart by rivalry."

"That's not going to happen, Ian. Children squabble, but they grow up to be the best of friends. Look at me and Grace."

As if she'd summoned her sister, a liveried footman announced, "Mr. and Mrs. Emerson have arrived, Your Grace. My lady."

Tavi seized her husband by the hand, and, laughing, went to welcome her sister in from the cold.

❄

Visit Ian and Tavi twelve years later -
get your steamy bonus epilogue:

THE DUKE'S CHRISTMAS SCANDAL

https://BookHip.com/HMDHGDN

❄

Thank you for reading The Duke's Christmas Scandal!
Please consider leaving a review on:
Amazon
GoodReads
Bookbub

AUTHOR'S NOTE & ACKNOWLEDGEMENTS

Most readers of historical romance are accustomed to inheritance laws of primogeniture, in which the eldest son inherits the entire estate.

But what happens when an elite family doesn't produce a male heir—which happened more than a quarter of the time?

The estate would go to another cousin male heir, and the daughter(s) would marry into another wealthy family a la Jane Austen's *Pride and Prejudice*, right?

Well, not always. It depends upon the how the letters of patent were written. I am deeply grateful to Isobel Carr for teaching a class on titles and inheritance through the Beau Monde's Regency Academy. I have wanted to do a story with a title gone into abeyance ever since I took her class, and this project offered the perfect opportunity to do so. The group of daughters co-inheriting a dukedom is a real thing that could have happened, and the application process is as described in this book.

I added the birthmark for humor, and partly because of a discussion where I realized there are multiple misunderstandings about what birthmarks are. They are skin markings that are either present

AUTHOR'S NOTE & ACKNOWLEDGEMENTS

at birth, or show soon thereafter. They may be vascular or pigmented. Some are inherited, and they can run in families.

In an era where DNA testing wasn't available, people relied upon physical features to determine lineage whenever there was doubt.

For Ian, that means proving his lineage with a painting of his forebears' bottom, and revealing his own before the Select Committee for Privileges.

You're welcome for that visual!

I hope you've enjoyed this romp through snowy 1816, the Year of No Summer. Thank you for reading *The Duke's Christmas Scandal*!

My thanks to the following people:

Eve Pendle, Anne Knight, and Ebony Oaten for early feedback on this story; Isobel Carr for teaching Inheriting an English Peerage; to the Beau Monde for making the Regency Academy available; to Charity Chimni for editing; to Zoe York for blurb feedback; and most especially to the members of the *How the Rake Stole Christmas* collaboration.

With love and gratitude to my family, and to every single one of my readers - I wouldn't be here without you.

Carrie Lomax

ABOUT THE AUTHOR

Carrie Lomax is the bestselling author of historical & contemporary romance. She also writes angsty new adult fantasy romance under the pen name Joline Pearce.

Growing up rural Wisconsin, she spent a lot of time roaming the woods and fantasizing about new places. Adventures took her to Oregon, Michigan, and after a stint teaching in France, she moved to New York City, where she stayed for the next 15 years. There she acquired a pair of graduate degrees, a husband and a career as a librarian. An avid runner, reader, and cyclist, she lives in Maryland with two budding readers and her real-life romantic hero.

BOOKS BY CARRIE LOMAX

Regency Historical Romance
I Like Big Dukes… (bestselling multi-author anthology)
-*The Duke She Defied*

-*The Spinster's Secret Scoundrel*

-*The Duke's Christmas Scandal (How the Rake Stole Christmas)*

The Wild Lord (London Scandals Book 1)
Becoming Lady Dalton (London Scandals Book 2)
The Lost Lord (London Scandals Book 3)
The Duke's Stolen Heart (London Scandals Book 4)

Twelve Nights of Scandal
Twelve Nights of Ruin
(Duet)

***Virtue & Vice* Victorian Historical Romance Series**
Belladonna
Annalise

BOOKS BY CARRIE LOMAX

Rosalyn
Justine

Forthcoming in the *Virtue & Vice* series (2024):
Cora
Isabelle
Rose
Jane

Contemporary series:
Say You'll Stay (Alyssa & Marc)
Say You Need Me (Janelle & Trent)
Say 'I Do' (Bonus Novella: Fiji Wedding)
Say You're Mine (Olivia & Ronan)

Fantasy Romance written as Joline Pearce:
Falling Princess
Eternal Knight
Queen Rising
Crimson Throne

Visit www.CarrieLomax.com for details & buy links